Just Business

Mustafa Kulle

Cover art by Mustafa Kulle
www.MustafaKulle.com

Acknowledgements

Special Thanks to my Editor Dr. Stephen Carver

Special Thanks to my family and friends for all their love and support.

I only met him a few times briefly. His name was Nicholas Kroll, or Nick as everyone else called him, he was known as a nice guy. He worked in the local charity shop from time to time, and he would help carry shopping bags for the elderly.

I even greeted him when I walked passed him on the street, he would flash me a smile and say "Hello" or "Good day to you sir" and then walk on. He just seemed normal. He looked good, white male in his mid-thirties, he was always well dressed, polite, quite a gentleman really, more like a goody two shoes who could do no harm. I can't believe I'm saying all this, describing him in such a way that it feels so absurd. Who could have known the kind of... creature... that he was? There was nothing human about him whatsoever. The very thought of him makes me shudder.

To push all that aside from my mind for now, I'll begin with the area I used to patrol working as a Bobby-on-the-Beat for the Metropolitan Police. Walker Grove is a quiet area in North London, it was a small village until the late 19th Century. When the London Underground became electrified it grew into a town. With a growing economy and mass immigration, the city of London grew so large that this town is now part of its suburban outer skirts. Surrounding the historical mansions built by aristocrats were neighbourhoods composed of streets with houses that were built in the 1930^s as part the British Art Deco Movement, until then Walker Grove was rural and undeveloped as it was used as the King's hunting grounds. Now it is a vibrant but peaceful area with shops, pubs, restaurants and cafes. Folk here are friendly, and well spoken.

Crime here is virtually non-existent, apart from the odd petty theft here, drunk and disorderly behaviour there, I can tell you this is one of the nicest areas of London, if not Britain, to live in. It is because of this reason that makes this case so shocking, so sickening; it's hard to believe it happened at all in such a place. It gets worse, this case has been classified; in other words, I am not allowed to breathe a word of this to anyone, which means the whole town doesn't know anything about it. It was never mentioned in the news either. As far as the locals are concerned, it was just a 'minor disturbance' as we have been told to tell them. And that was it. It was never spoken of again.

I saw his place for myself. The house was a semi-detached built in the 1930^s, with a custom loft conversion and a basement, all constructed without permission or the council's consent. Most likely constructed by hired migrant workers to do the job as they didn't give a damn about regulations as long as it filled their pockets with cash, and their services were cheap too.

I was refused access at first to gain access to the house, so I had to pester a lot of my colleagues in secret time and time again until eventually I was given an 'exceptional' permission to investigate the premises, but I was not allowed to go alone, I was only to be accompanied by members of the forensic team to make sure I didn't tamper with the evidence or take anything. That was fine by me.

We went there at 5:38 in the morning, two forensics came with me in a patrol car. We parked it in front of the house. Thankfully it was daylight enough to see as it was spring.

From the outside it looks just like any other house you wouldn't give a second glance to. It's a two bedroom semi-detached house with art deco features built in the 1930^s. The two forensics urged me out of the car and they complained that we shouldn't be here and we shouldn't spend too long either. At their suggestion we started by going upstairs.

To access the attic, there was a concealed custom-built staircase that can be lowered from the ceiling. I took a deep breath, and then went up to have a look. There wasn't much to see except for the disturbed surfaces of the wooden beams holding the roof. He had tied the women up with rope and wire so tightly that no one could break free. I looked around and I spotted two surveillance cameras. That way he kept an eye on them.

When we explored the upstairs, there was nothing out of the ordinary in the bedroom or the bathroom.
But when we entered the second bedroom, it was anything but. It was the computer room, his lab. I had never seen anything like it; it was as if I entered a CCTV camera room. This was where he spent most of his time.

As soon as I entered it was dark, my colleague turned on the light. The window that faced the back garden was boarded up with chipboard, concealing the room from the view outside completely, the only source of light in this room was the bare light bulb hanging from the ceiling.

He had 12 monitors attached to his computer. The

computer itself was attached to a server that had all the cameras connected to it, and this is where all the footage would be recorded. Using the computer attached to it, he would extract the desired video footage from the server to edit them using video editing software, this is where he made 'movies' out of everything he recorded. But there was something wrong, his computer had been opened and taken apart. The hard drives which stored that data were missing. When I asked one of the forensics, they said they had taken them in for evidence. They couldn't give any details.

Behind the server was a thick rope made of wires. Two of the wires came from the ceiling which I understood to be connected to the surveillance cameras upstairs in the attic. The rest went through a hole in the floor located in the corner of the room. The rest of the wires were all attached to the monitors. Arranged in some sort of grid, like a wall of screens tiled next to each other on top of a desk. They curved out into a crescent shape. On his desk lay a keyboard, a mouse, a microphone, and high quality speakers. And right in front of the desk was his black leather desk chair.

His chair, keyboard, mouse, the floor surrounding the chair, the front part of the surface of the desk was covered in dried semen. Whatever he saw on those screens aroused him to masturbate more regularly than normal. At the rate he did, it was enough to fill a paint bucket each week. I've known people who watch porn for hours and maintain good hygiene, but this was a sick sight.

His computer had four slots that housed DVD and Blu-ray re-writers that burned the videos he made on to the disks. Next to his desk were stacks of blank DVD and Blu-ray disks, and empty cases for them.

At the back of the room was a large 52-inch HD television, attached to a Blu-ray and DVD player. I guessed this would be his quality control phase, to test his movies on disk, on a big screen before selling them to his customers. Making sure his videos worked perfectly before packing them up, and shipping them to his customers around the world. Whoever they are must be real sickos who need their heads examined, and deserve to be locked up.

Under his desk was a safe, that was left wide open which indicated that it was emptied recently, I figured that was where he stored the cash he made from selling these disks. When I enquired how much was in it, the forensic team said they didn't know. Funny, they're the ones who collect the evidence.

One entire wall was a shelf, but it was also empty and all its contents were removed recently. When I asked the forensic team what was in it, they said they didn't know. Yeah right. They were lying to my face.

In the other corner of the room was a microwave on a table, and next to the table was a bin full of boxes made of card, plastic, plastic film, and foil, piled up in the bin and spilling out over the edges. All he ate was microwave meals. So he didn't need to leave the room to eat.

I sighed and decided to leave the room and go downstairs. The kitchen was spotless, mostly unused with empty cupboards. Who needs a kitchen when you live on microwave meals anyway? Apart from the milk in the fridge he used for the cereals, the room was bare and clean.

The living room was a perfect modern lounge, the sort you would see in a furniture advert on television, or one of those flashy interior design programmes. Laminated flooring throughout the ground floor, empty plain furniture, leather couches and armchairs, all unused. No framed pictures on walls. Nothing suspicious here.

The basement was a different story.

"You sure you want to go in there?" asked one of the forensics.

"Yes" I insisted. They tutted. They sighed. They urged me to be quick. Having already come this far, I prepared for the worst. They gave me a torch. There was a cupboard under the stairs, inside there was another door but concealed. Upon opening it we descended down the stairs. This was also custom built. No way the council would have approved of this construction. We turned on the light in the stairway. Once we reached the basement floor, we approached another door. We opened it. There was a sudden whiff of a ghastly smell that made me gag. It stank of blood. It was dark, so we took out our torches and began to scan the area with our beams of light. We entered a room where there was a shower and lots of cleaning materials like bleach, disinfectants, whiteners, and other household chemicals. There were bloodstains all over the floor. I guessed this is where he would clean up before going upstairs. In the corner of the room was a workbench with an axe, meat cleavers, and other cutting equipment with rolls of bin liners under it. I understood this was how he disposed of the bodies.

And right in front of us was another door. It had a drawing of a spiral of blood smeared on it by hand. This was it.

The "Games" room. Despite the bad smell in this room, I tried to take a deep breath before going in. We opened the door. It was pitch black; and the stench was even worse. It was so strong I had to take out a tissue to cover my mouth and nose with it. I looked around the room as I shone the light of my torch around. Like a spotlight in a theatre, my torch revealed all to me in only small circles as I moved my torch in slow sweeping motions. Looking up and down, left and right.

The floor was sticky and thick with dried blood. As we stepped around the room, it felt like walking on thick mud, the blood on the floor was so sticky we had to lift our feet from the ground with a bit of effort.

The sight was horrifying. I looked on the floor I saw mutilated body parts; intestines, stomachs, muscles, brains... anything that's supposed to stay within one's skin was found scattered on the floor. I couldn't bear the sight so I kept my head up. There was a range of objects hanging on the blood splattered walls; crowbars, hammers, axes, knives, glass shards, sickles, scalpels, machetes, baseball bats, chains, and metal wire. There are cameras everywhere, in every corner of the room and at various angles. I had no doubt in my mind at all that each of these cameras were displayed on Nick's monitors, to be stored on to his server, and later edited on his computer upstairs. There was no lighting here because the florescent lights had been smashed.

Above the doorway there was a small dome shaped surveillance camera. Next to it was a small speaker. This must be what he used to tell the "players" what to do from his microphone.

The walls were just plasterboards painted with white emulsion paint, but the white had been splattered with blood in every direction, even the white ceiling. On each wall were individual coat hangers that held a weapon or a tool. It was clear that many fights took place in this room with those objects in hand.

I've never been so nauseated in my life, I was beginning to feel physically sick so I excused myself and went back up the stairs and out through the front door. I had seen enough. The weather was cold and grey, but the breeze gave me a liberating sense of gratitude that I was still alive. It made me feel so much better. The fresh air brought me back to my senses.

I waited outside for the forensics team to come out and join me. They asked me if I was OK, I told them I was fine. We got into the patrol car and they drove me back to the station.

I tried to continue my investigation into this case but it wasn't as straightforward as I expected it to be.

Everyone was being adamantly discreet about this as if nobody knew anything, as if it never happened.

Even my good friends whom I worked with for many years were hesitant and reluctant to help. Only one of them, Tim, accidentally let it slip that I wasn't supposed to "know" any of this. When I pressed him, he revealed to me that there has been a sort of "cover up". I couldn't believe my ears, nor understand why I wasn't told about any of this. My colleague insisted the less I knew the better. I wasn't convinced.

I told him that I saw the empty shelf, the emptied safe, and the computer with the missing hard drives. To which he admitted that the police had taken them in for "evidence". I wanted to confirm my findings.

When I asked him what was in the shelf, he told me that it was Nick's entire library of all the videos and movies he made, some of them were his "personal favourites" he never sold but kept for himself. All of them were taken in for evidence.

Then I enquired about the safe, my colleague told me that was where he stored all the cash. When I asked how much, he couldn't give me an exact figure, he just said "thousands of pounds worth of cash". He then explained that this hobby of his was also his job, hence such an income.

When I asked him what was in those hard drives, he told me that it not only contained the edited footage, but all the names, addresses and account details of all his customers who ordered those movies he made from him over the internet. He had customers all over the world, Europe, America, and Asia. But the vast majority of these sick minded people were living right here in the UK. Nick had hundreds of customers. I asked for their details to which he refused, then he pointed out that the revealing the names of the recipients would violate the protection of their personal data, therefore had to remain classified. Bollocks! This trade isn't even legal, and yet the police are protecting the identities of people who purchased illegally made snuff films?

I asked Tim for more information but still he was hesitant, and seemed reluctant to assist any further. My curiosity got the better of me, so I feebly begged him for the details of the victims he killed. I had to know if they were among the locals I see everyday. Tim sighed and he said he will see what he can do for me, but then he warned "You don't realise what you're getting in to." Then we made a mutual agreement to keep this between ourselves. At that moment I asked him if he saw any of the footage for himself. He nodded. I asked him if I could watch them, but it "wasn't possible".

And he was right, I wasn't allowed in the department. After all, it was his job to analyse evidence in the police department. He was one of the officers who would spend hours analysing video footage. Most of it was CCTV footage caught during thefts and assaults, but sometimes it was child porn, and domestic violence, and rape. They would watch children under the age of 18 being raped and beaten in graphic detail. How on earth do they endure watching such things on a daily a basis? It's beyond me.

Then I pointed out to him that I was hoping perhaps I would understand why a person would do such things, and try and come to an understanding as to what causes such actions. Based on what I've seen so far. I cannot bear to not know. If I don't find out, it will not let me rest. I know that if I don't find out, I will be wondering for the rest of my life. Maybe this will put my mind at ease.

The next day, was my day off, I received a phone call from Tim that he was coming from the station to drop off a folder. I carefully opened it and I found the information about Nicolas Kroll's latest victims. As I scanned through them, I saw their photos and histories.

I guessed this is everything I needed. A part of me was beginning to think this was a bad idea, as if I was about to open Pandora's box. But I had to know. He didn't say a word, after he left I placed the folder on my coffee table, sat on my sofa with my cup of coffee, and took out the documents to read. At least none of the victims were anyone I knew in Walker Grove, but it was still a saddening experience reading about these poor girls:

Maxine Elliot, aged 22, she was a single mum who worked in a beauty salon somewhere in the north east of London. She lived in an area that was quite rough compared to the likes of Walker Grove. She has a two-year-old girl who has been taken into care and still doesn't know what happened to her mother. Maxine was struggling to make ends meet with her poorly paid job and the flat she couldn't afford to stay in, the greedy landlord didn't care about her circumstances and kept increasing the rent. Prostitution was her other job which provided her with extra cash to stay financially afloat.

Michelle Garber, aged 18, a college student who ran away from home. She wanted to leave college to become a model but her parents wouldn't let her. With nowhere to stay and no job, she took up the job of being a call girl.

Stacey Jillian, aged 32, worked in a cafe until she had lost her job when her manager ended an affair he had with her. She was forced to have a sexual relationship with her employer against her will. The only reason he spent so much time away from home was to stay at work to have sex with Stacey. One day his wife found out about the affair and gave him an ultimatum. She was fired and left with nothing. She became a prostitute in order to get by.

I put the documents down on the table for a moment to reflect on what I've read. I closed my eyes and massaged my eye sockets with my thumb and forefinger. My sympathy for these girls made me think about my own daughter. She's 13 now, but I haven't seen her for nearly 3 years since my partner Kathy and I separated as I couldn't spend time with my family. They moved to live in Edinburgh where the rest of my ex-partner's family was. At the time I couldn't go with them, a transfer wasn't possible either. I sighed and then realised that I hadn't finished my coffee and it had gone cold. I did not want anymore coffee. I took out the other documents and read the last two victims.

Emily Williams, Aged 24, worked in retail on a zero-hour contract. Having no work for weeks on end she had to find another job. On top of that, she was bullied by scolding lazy managers who increased her workload and cut her pay. She was forced to resign.

She worked as a waitress that was just as bad. It was meant to be part time, the hours and the pay were not enough to live on. So she took on a second job as a bar maid, but it still wasn't enough.

She never got a stable job that was neither full time nor paid a decent living wage. She was denied welfare. So in her desperation she turned to prostitution, as this was the only job that was consistent and paid far better than any other job she applied for.

She would make £100 per hour as an escort, that paid her far more than any job she had. While any other job barely paid the minimum wage, had uncertain hours, and no job security.

Holly Abbot, Aged 19, grew up in a care home where she was repeatedly raped by the carers in Yorkshire. She ran away from the care home and became a prostitute, getting by living in hostels. She wanted to become a model, but due to high competition and a saturated market, she got rejected every time. Having been exploited and shunned, this seemed the only thing that gave her a chance to get by in life. Later on she turned to drugs and prostitution.

Each of these women were young and beautiful, with whole lives ahead of them. But who would have known or prevented them from having their lives end in such horrific ways?

Having read everything, I put all the documents down on to the coffee table. At this point I became depressed. I was beginning to think maybe I should reconsider my career and change jobs or something. No, brush that aside for now.

When I flipped over the last page, I found two small plastic sleeves holding a DVD in them. On one of the sleeves was a note from my colleague that said "For your eyes only, Destroy after use." He had made copies of them instead of taking the originals. These were the last two movies that Nick made. And all the data in the folder he gave me containing the victims' data were the victims featured in the DVDs. I slipped open the two sleeves. I found another note;

"Are you sure you want to see this? There is no going back. Think about it."

Holding the disks in my hands, I had a moment of dilemma: should I or should I not? Well, why not? After all, this was some sicko who had a strange fetish. I'm a policeman, my job is to solve crime and fight for justice. I had to know.

And so I place the first disk into my DVD player, pressed the play button and began to watch.

The first thing I saw was the games room. Three prostitutes were laying on the floor, Maxine, Michelle and Stacey. They were beaten black and blue by Nick earlier. I couldn't work out if they were asleep or not. The room was well lit thanks to the florescent lights. But the floor and the walls were still splattered with blood.

"Wakey wakey. Breakfast is ready." A voice spoke mockingly. It was Nick. I knew it was coming from the speaker above the door.

The girls were stricken with fear as they awoke, terrified by their surroundings. They rose to their feet looking around in dismay.

"What is this place?" Maxine shrieked.

"What's going on?" Michelle panicked.

"Get me out of here!" Stacey screamed.

"Hello girls. You are now going to play a little game." Nick began. "It's 'Kill or be Killed', I'm only going to let one of you go. And that'll be your prize. The rules are simple. To survive, you have to kill one another until only one of you is standing. If you want to get out of here, you're going to have to fight for your life.

Don't think you can sit this one out. I injected you all with a slow acting poison that will kill you within an hour. I only have enough antidote for one. So you better hurry.

Oh, and another thing, this game won't be fun empty handed so I placed some goodies around just for you. Remember, you're playing for the camera. So try and make this look fun. Let the game begin."

The three prostitutes look at each other in fear for a split second, and they run in opposite directions to seize a weapon each. Michelle grabbed a machete, Maxine grabbed an axe, and Stacey grabbed a baseball bat. Then they faced each other clinging on to their weapons in self defence.

Maxine starts waving the axe around to keep the others away from her. Michelle cowers back into a corner, holding onto the machete with her life. Stacey is standing in the middle of the room holding the bat ready for a swing. Looking at both girls;

"Come on! What are you waiting for!?" she shouts.

"Please, I don't want to do this," said Michelle, breaking down to tears as she presses her back to the corner and slides into sitting on the floor.

"I've been here longer than both of you, I'm the one who should leave," said Stacey.

"Not without a fight," said Maxine.

"Let's do this!" Stacey runs at Maxine, swinging the baseball bat around as Maxine dodges. After several attempts with the bat, Maxine dodges and tries to cut Stacey vertically with the axe, but she misses and loses her balance, Stacey hits her back and hits her again and again with the baseball bat, breaking her every bone, before hitting her head, creating a devastating execution. Maxine's head was all mashed up and her blood was all over the floor, spreading wildly like a growing puddle in the rain. Stacey is breathing heavily to regain her strength as she stares at the fresh corpse of Maxine.

This whole video was presented in different camera angles, cutting from one angle to another, zooming in and out. It was clear that Nick was playing director and cameraman whilst watching this in action on his monitors. I hate to say it, but he has quite a talent for editing and cinematography. It would have entertaining if it wasn't so sick. No wonder he had so many customers. He clearly enjoyed what he was doing and this all must have been thrilling to him.

Michelle was crying her eyes out in fear, gritting her teeth, and trembling.

"Oh my god... oh my god...oh my god" She mumbled to herself. Stacey pulled herself up with the bat in both hands and slowly turns to Michelle before walking to towards her.

"I know how it feels, but I promise this won't hurt one bit if you just don't move" said Stacey.
Clutching her machete tight, Michelle is still on her knees, shaking.

"Please...please don't," she begged.

"I'm sorry, but this is the only way. I don't want to do this either, " said Stacey as she approaches Michelle closer and closer.

"No! Please don't." cried Michelle.
"It'll be over soon, trust me, now hold still," Stacey stands over Michelle, places the bat over Michelle's head, sticky with thick blood with a ghastly smell. Stacey raises the bat over her head ready for the final swing with both hands...

"NOOOOOOO!!!" Michelle leaps forward, plunging the machete through Stacey's chest with all her strength. Stacey is in a state of shock, with no strength to hold the bat anymore she drops it. Michelle is still holding on to the machete with both hands, she couldn't pull it out. She lets go, allowing Stacey to fall to the ground with it. Michelle is shaking like mad, and falls to her knees crying and begins to scream out her painful guilt. Michelle continues to cry while she whispered "I'm sorry."

At this point, the basement door slowly creaks open. She's now free to go. Feeling weak from this entire trauma, Michelle picks herself up to make her way to the door when suddenly a dark figure appeared at the doorway with a loud roar of what sounds like a motor. It was Nick with a chainsaw!

"We have a winner!" he gleefully shouted as he ran towards her like a mad man. With nowhere to run, Michelle screams as she attempts to run away from him but Nick is too fast for her. With his eyes wide open, a big grin on his face from ear to ear, he mutilates Michelle to pieces as she screams. Waving around the chainsaw held tightly, blood would splat everywhere, her limbs fly off and then he starts to plunge the chainsaw into her mutilated body in a stabbing motion again and again. He's now getting tired; he turns off the chainsaw, and drags himself out of the basement and back into his computer room, slamming the basement door shut behind him.

My DVD player stopped playing as the film ended. This was just one of the many videos he made out of killing innocent women. I felt like throwing up. I could not comprehend the kind of people who view this as a source of entertainment. Monsters? Maniacs? No, worse. I don't think any words can describe them.

At this point I needed a break. I went outside into my back garden, I needed to breath. The cool air was soothing. I looked up and saw the sky was as grey as this morning when I woke up, the weather was cold and grey. Typical, grey in the day, black at night. I could do with some sunshine. Hell, I could do with a holiday. For now I can settle for a cigarette. Took one out of a pack, lit it, and then took in a deep breath. I tried to quit. It's not as easy as they say. At least it helps me cope with my work. I looked around my garden, it was only then when it dawned on me how much I've neglected it. The grass is tall as I hadn't mowed the lawn. All vegetation is overgrown, accompanied by dead flowers from seasons come and gone. Kathy and I used to do the gardening together on sunny days. I never looked at the garden since she left.

Maybe I'll make a start some day. Even on days I have off work, there isn't much for me to do. All my friends are at work. So I might as well keep myself busy somehow. Truth be told, I think the house needs redecorating. Nah, I don't know, I guess I'm trying to take my mind off things. Anyway, my cigarette finished, so I threw the butt on the stone patio pathway and went back inside as the weather became cooler.

I picked up the other DVD and took a deep breath as I replaced it with the other one I just watched. I braced myself as I picked up the remote and pressed play.

The film began all dark, nothing can be seen. But there is a constant sound of banging as if someone was rapidly pounding a door with fists hard in a desperate attempt to get out. "Get me out of here!" a voice screamed.

It was one of the two prostitutes. It wasn't certain which one it was until the florescent lights were turned on to reveal the room she was in. It was Emily.

"Oh my god!" she shrieked. "What the fuck is this?!"

There was another woman lying down in the middle of the floor. She looked as if she had been severely beaten up and probably raped prior to the shooting of this film. She lay there crying in agony.

"Holly? Holly?! Oh my god!!!" Emily cried. She rushed over to the girl, fell to her knees and held Holly in her arms like a baby. Unlike the women in the previous video, it seemed like they knew each other.

Emily looked around her, terrorised by the sight of the blood splattered walls and all the weapons were neatly placed back on the walls again, hanging and ready.

"What is this place?" she sobbed in rage.

A taunting voice came from the speaker again.

"What a touching moment? True friends are always there

for each other, even until death," Nick laughed, "We're going to play a little game. Unfortunately, one of you is going to have to die. But this should be easy enough, your friend is weak, so all you have to do is to kill her and you'll be free."

"No way!" Emily bellowed.

"Oh yes there is a way. It's the only one way out for you and that is to kill her. Otherwise the slow acting poison in your veins will kill you within an hour. You kill her you live, it's that simple."

"And look," he continued, "you have a whole variety of ways to kill your precious friend. So how will you do it? Put her out of her misery with a swift kill? Or you could give her a slow tortuous death for the camera, say cheese," said Nick as he laughed. "Now get going. Entertain me! We haven't got all night."

In despair Holly bursts into tears. Emily stands up, looks around and spots some of the cameras. Emily then runs over to the wall where a crowbar and a machete are hanging. She grabs the crowbar and the machete, then she runs over to each and every florescent light and smashes them with the crowbar. The room is instantly darkened. Nothing can be seen.

The sounds were very faint so I turned up the volume so I could hear them better.

From what I could hear, it sounded like Emily walked over to Holly, knelt down and whispered something to her ear. I couldn't hear what she was saying, it was at this point that I paused the video, rewind it a few seconds, and turn up the volume more. As the video played, I heard a very faint whisper from Emily to Holly. I think she said "Don't worry, I'm getting us out of here." Afterwards Emily left Holly on the sticky blood splattered floor. She got up and moved, but I couldn't tell where.

There is a long eerie silence until footsteps and a strange noise were heard coming towards the door. The door swings open, light from a torch beams out into the room, it slowly moves around and makes its way to reveal Holly still laying on the floor, crying.

Nick steps into the basement to approach Holly. Nick is holding his chainsaw with a torch attached to it with duct tape so that he can hold the chainsaw with both hands and illuminate his path at the same time. Nick slowly walks towards Holly when suddenly his hands are hacked off with a machete at the sound of an ear-piercing scream, followed by Nick's screaming in agony. It was Emily hacking away at Nick like a mad woman in absolute terror and rage.

The screams were so loud it made me jump. I cursed as I forgot to turn the volume down. It made me tremble. I seized the remote control to pause the video to turn it down. My heart was racing so hard I felt it thumping my chest. I took a few deep breaths to recollect myself before pressing Play again.

The chainsaw falls to the floor and spins around for the torch to reveal all that was happening. Emily was screaming as she kept hitting Nick with the machete. Nick's hands were missing but his arms were swinging all over the place helpless as he couldn't see nor defend himself, he cowered as he screamed in pain. She carries on slashing at Nick with the machete until he falls to the ground. Emily throws the machete a side, runs to the chainsaw, grabs it and then she jabs the whirring blades of the chainsaw into Nick's body again and again and again. To finish him off, with all her might she thrusts the chainsaw into his face and then cutting him to pieces. Nick is dead. Emily stands over his corpse, panting to regain her breath, and perhaps her sanity. She puts the chainsaw down, removes the torch and heads over to help Holly.

"Come on! Were getting out." Emily takes Holly's arm and puts it over her shoulder as she lifts her up.

Just then a loud banging could be heard from outside the basement accompanied by the sound of heavy feet running followed by the sound of men shouting "Met Police! Nobody move!" It was the Specialist Firearms Command, a whole team of CO-19 officers were deployed.

"HELP! WE'RE DOWN HERE!" Emily screamed.

The CO-19 officers ran down the stairs in to the basement, holding torches and armed with Heckler & Kock MP5 9mm (MP5A3) submachine guns. Fingers on triggers ready to fire, they bellowed their commands;

"Don't move!"

"You're under arrest!"

"Hold it right there!"

Emily couldn't say anything, she looked caught off guard and confused. More armed officers ran into the basement, they grabbed the two girls and immediately hand-cuffed them. The girls protested resisting arrest when they were hit on their heads with truncheons. Soon the CO-19 Officers and the girls went up the stairs and vanished into the pitch black darkness.

It was at that point the video ended. It didn't make any sense. Nick is dead. If Nick didn't make this video, then who did? How did my colleague Tim get hold of this movie? So the whole time Nick wasn't working alone? If so why didn't anybody tell me? Where are the girls now? They must still be alive! Where are they? My mind was overloaded with questions. I was itching to do something.

I couldn't help myself, I had to get to the bottom of this. My first instinct was to go to the house. Don't know why. Something was telling me to go there. I grabbed my coat and my keys before rushing over to the house where Nick lived. To my horror I saw a crew of builders and construction workers coming in and out of the house. The place was cordoned off. I parked my car, got out and confronted the builders.

"Hey! What are you doing?!" I shouted.

At first the workers were puzzled, briefly looked at one another and carried on working.

One of the workers came out of the front door, I stopped him in his tracks.

"This is a crime scene! You're destroying evidence of unsolved murders!"

He waved his arms at me in a 'go away' manner.

"No no," he said in an eastern European accent. "This is essential maintenance and repairs."

Lies! I know it is. I tried to enter the building but four of the muscular workers blocked my way. They surrounded me like a gang of gorillas ready to pounce of me. I showed them my badge. I tried to stay calm. But this was madness.

"I'm a policeman," I said, "who authorised this?"

"You did, the police," one of the workers replied.

"What?! No! This is a crime scene," I couldn't believe it.

"They didn't tell us that," another replied. "We were told by the council to 'rejuvenate' the premises. And you, the police, approved it."

"That can't be right. Let me go in." I tried again.

"Not without permission." The workers closed in on me blocking my path tighter. To which I grunted.

I went back to my car and I raced over to the station. I got out of the car and the first person I wanted to see was Tim. I was greeted by a few of my other colleagues who were surprised to see me on my day off.

"Where's Tim?" I asked.

"He just came in." One of my colleagues replied. Then he must be in the locker room. I found him. He was alone. He had just put on his holster. He saw me and said nothing. As soon as I caught sight of him I marched right up to him.

"Holly and Emily! Where are they?" I demanded to know. "Who?" He asked.

"Cut the crap!" I went up to his face. "There are builders in that house. Why?"

"I don't know." He said.

My mind went blank. I grabbed him and pushed him against the wall. I clenched my fists around his collar bones, pressing him harder into the wall.

"Don't be stupid." He tried to fight back.

"Oh yeah!" I growled through my gritted teeth. I pulled him towards me and pushed him back into the wall even harder. I wrestled with him. After a quick struggle I pulled the gun out from his holster and pressed the nozzle into his neck. I was ready to blow his brains out.

"Go on then." Tim looked at me like I wouldn't dare. I pulled the hammer of the pistol back until it clicked into place. I pushed the gun harder into his neck. I saw the pupils in his eyes widen. His breathing became as frantic as mine. "You fucking maniac."

"You're part of this." I growled.

"You're wrong. You know as much as I do."

"Bullshit!" I bellowed. "You knew all along didn't you."

"I told you I don't know." Tim lied again.

"You expect me to believe that? Eh? Let's go outside and

broadcast it then. Shall we? Eh?" I uttered. My chest was aching by the rapid hammering of my heart. My muscles were stiff. We glared at one another as we breathed through our flaring nostrils.

"Get your hands off me or I will report you for assault." Tim's voice was shaky.

"Not before I report you first. For giving me those files." I meant it. I was ready to lose my job over this. But he wasn't. Not with a wife and a kid to feed.

"To the cleaners' room. Now." That did it. Tim finally gave in.

I slowly loosened my grip. The thumb of my hand holding the gun pushed the hammer back to its original place. I backed away from him breathing heavily. The rushing of adrenaline made us tired. My chest was hurting from all that stress. I gave Tim back his gun which he placed into his holster.

He lead the way, and we walked into the cleaner's room. Nobody was in. The coast was clear. It was a small room where all the cleaning utilities were. It stank of bleach and disinfectants. It reminded me of the cleaning area just before the doorway of Nick's "Games" room. The stench brought back all the sights and smells from that hunted house all at once and it made me gag. At least there was a light above, but it was dim dirty. At least it gave us the privacy we needed. It was just Tim and me.

Tim sighed and began to explain. I was not prepared to hear what he told me. At the end of it all, it left me flabbergasted. Sickened. And... and... mad.

"Nicholas Kroll was working for the Metropolitan Police the whole time," Tim started.

I was shocked.

"Why would they hire him?" I asked.

"It seemed he was a suitable candidate for the job. He was a cold-blooded psychopath, a convicted rapist, a paedophile, a sadistic serial killer... and he was obsessed with snuff films. He was good with editing. He liked making movies."

"But why? Why not just lock him up?"

"No amount of rehab would have helped this guy. And keeping him in prison won't do anyone any good. It will just be a waste of his talent, let alone tax payer's money."

"Will you listen to yourself? You sound like a fan of his."

"Look, I'm only doing what I think is best for my country."

"Bullshit!" I blasted. "You can just put him out of his misery."

"Euthanasia? Huh! That's still illegal you know. What do you want? The electric chair? What makes that more legal than the other. Besides, there is a lot of money to be made out of this. With all the cuts the government's been imposing on us lately. We need all the cash we can get."

"So all that was for money?" I didn't know whether to laugh or cry.

"Why not? There is a market for that kind of material. We have customers all over the world, let alone in this country. The police, government officials, senior figureheads, the media," Tim continued, "you know as well as I do, for all the obvious reasons we can't allow this to be available to the public. Otherwise everyone else will be killing on the streets and posting their crude stuff on the internet."

"Ultimately putting you out of business." I smirked.

"Is that what you want?"

"No!"

"Well someone's got to do it, you know. Who can do this better than the police? Hmm?" Tim went up in my face.

He allowed a pause for it all to sink in. But it was just the beginning.

"So who was he? Nick?" I asked.

"Nobody knows. He was given a new identity, relocated, the rest of his history was erased."

"What about the house?" I enquired, "The builders said something about an 'approval' from the council and the police."

"That's right. You see, the council played a role in giving

him a house to live in and provided illegal customisations in order to make a living out of his hobby, which was also his new job. After killing the prostitutes we would assist him in his disposal of the bodies." Tim was casual in his explanation, he seemed so relaxed about it. "And as for the house now, well, once the rejuvenation is complete, it will be sold to the public. The new occupants will never know."

"Clever bastards," I whispered. "So how many did he kill?"

"We don't know the total death toll, but my guess is in the hundreds. From what I can tell, we may never know."

"So where are the girls now? Emily and Holly. The last victims."

"They're dead."

"No way! I saw the footage. They were arrested. The CO-19 officers captured them."

"They were taken to the woods to be executed." Tim paused briefly. "You know we can't have witnesses."

My mouth trembled when my jaw dropped. "You? The police... killed them? Oh my god."

I never felt so betrayed. I was losing myself. Feeling weak I leaned against the wall. I massaged my eye sockets with my index finger and my thumb. I tried to steady my breathing but I couldn't help it. I turned to face the wall, buried my head in my arms and sobbed.

Tim stood still, he crossed his arms, rolled his eyes, and sighed while giving me time for all this to sink in. I wasn't sure how much more of this I could take. I took a few more deep breaths.

"But... then..." I began, "how did... how did the police know what was going on that night?"

"After Emily smashed the lights in the basement he couldn't see what was going on. So he called the CO-19 officers for back-up. We told him to wait for us to come over and collect the girls, but he didn't do as he was told. That blundered."

"So what happens now?" I asked, "I mean the girls... now that they're dead we're going to have to tell their families."

"We're not going to." Said Tim, his voice was cold.

"What?!"

"They've been reported missing already." Tim paused briefly, "You see, when Nick imprisoned them in his attic, we waited for three weeks, until their friends and family came forward and reported them missing. The 'Missing' file went out. But that's fine. No one is going to find someone who's already dead. If we said nothing at all it would only arouse more suspicion. Once the girls' 'missing' status was announced to the public, that would be the right time for the filming to begin. They will never be seen again."

"So you knowingly tell the families of the missing you'll search for them when the whole time you actually have them detained? Why?"

"Like I said, we can't have witnesses. The victims know where the house is. They know what our man looks like. Letting them go is too risky. We can't have them speaking out."

"But they are dead now. Why not tell their families?"

"As far as the police are concerned, the 'Missing' cases are on hold. The families of the missing will be kept in the dark about the truth of their whereabouts for "as long as necessary". They will never be told the truth."

"This is madness." I growled. My blood was boiling.

Tim sighed again.

"Look. I know you don't believe in what we're doing. But I think in time you will appreciate the impact we are making. With such horror stories of girls going missing will discourage girls from getting into prostitution. So in a way we're doing the community a favour."

"You are sick," I uttered through gritted teeth.

"We are good cops." Tim answered.

"Shut up! I'm not like you!"

"Hold on. I'm not the one responsible for any of this. I'm just doing what I'm told. If I don't like it I can always quit. It wasn't exactly what I signed up for but what can you do?" Tim made it all sound so rational. I couldn't believe the shit he kept coming out with. As if he's been doing this for years. He sounded like a pro.

"So that's it then. It's all over." I hoped.

"What is?" Tim raised an eyebrow.

"This. All of this. Nick is dead. The victims are dead. No-one's going to know anyway. The house is being redone. So that's it. It's all over."

"No way." Said Tim in a very cold voice.

"What the hell are you talking about?"

"We've made far too much money from all this. We're not just going to give it all up. We have demands of customers to meet."

"No! You can't!"

"It's already began."

"What do you mean?"

"It's all being arranged as we speak," said Tim. "We have a new recruit. We are in the process of giving him a new identity, and customising a new house elsewhere. We're starting from scratch."

"How can you do this?!" I exclaimed.

"As easily as we did before."

"NO!"

As if he predicted my every move, I was just about to lunge forward at him when suddenly he took his gun out and pointed it at my face.

"This time the joke's on you, pal. I can blow your head off right here. We can make another cover up. No one will give a shit about you."

"So you really are behind all this. Why? We've been working together for years."

"It puts the cash my pocket."

"I should have known."

"Oh well. Too bad. Looks like you won't be benefiting from our private scheme after all." Tim smirked. "Look at you, you're not fit to participate."

"I don't want to."

"Doesn't matter. You know too much. It's up to you now. I could let you go, but, if you say a single word to anyone, there will be dire consequences for you and your family. Do you understand that?"

I nodded in a feeble way.

"You better watch your back, because moving forward we're going to be monitoring you. Everything you say and do will be under the tightest surveillance possible."

I was flabbergasted. Never in my life have I ever been so nauseated. My head was spinning, with all this coming together, I was beginning to feel dizzy. With this despicable level of corruption and cover-ups, I began to fear for my daughter's life. Career be damned!

“I don’t want any part of this.” I scorned.

“Good.”

“I mean it. I want to move to Scotland. I’m done with all this. If I can’t get a transfer, I’ll be handing in my letter of resignation tomorrow morning.” It was at that moment my decision to move to Edinburgh was more clear than before, where I can be with my little girl and make sure she never suffers the same fate as all the other girls who were killed.

“Very well.” Tim finally lowered his gun and put it back in his holster. “We’ll see what we can do.”

Just before we were about exit the cleaners’ room, I finally asked the one question:
“Why?”

The only answer I got, whether this was regarded as a crime or not, it was “just business”.